Miss Klute Is a Hoot!

Dan Gutman

Pictures by
Jim Paillot

SCHOLASTIC INC.

To Nicole Lynch

Thanks to Judy Hutnik, Chris Emerson, Laney Richardson Berry, Julie Ruminer, and Laurie Berkinshaw Skaggs

ISBN 978-0-545-79607-1

Text copyright © 2014 by Dan Gutman. Illustrations copyright © 2014 by Jim Paillot. All rights reserved. Published by Scholastic Inc., 557 Broadway, New York, NY 10012, by arrangement with HarperCollins Children's Books, a division of HarperCollins Publishers. SCHOLASTIC and associated logos are trademarks and/or registered trademarks of Scholastic Inc.

12 11 10 9 8 7 6 5 4 3 2 1   14 15 16 17 18 19/0

Printed in the U.S.A.   40

First Scholastic printing, November 2014

Typography by Kate Engbring

Contents

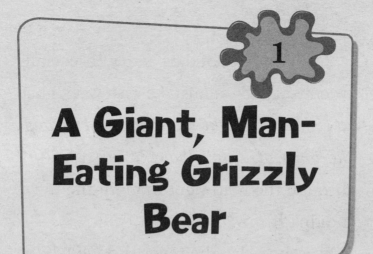

A Giant, Man-Eating Grizzly Bear

My name is A.J. and I hate reading out loud.

Every day in Mr. Granite's class, we have ROL time—Reading Out Loud. Each of us has to stand up and read a paragraph from a book in front of the whole class.*

---

*We're not even allowed to read out loud *loud*. If I read out loud *too* loud, Mr. Granite holds up his hand and makes a peace sign, which means "shut up."

Reading out loud is scary, especially when you make a mistake. Last week I had to read: *"I thought the road went through the town. It didn't though."* But I said, "I through the road went thought the town. It didn't throw."

Everybody laughed even though I didn't say anything funny.

"What a dumbhead!" whispered Andrea Young, this annoying girl with curly brown hair.

Hey, I'm not a dumbhead. The guy who decided how to spell "thought" and "through" and "though" was the dumbhead.

I was going to say something mean to

Andrea, but I didn't get the chance. You'll never believe who poked his head into the door at that moment.

Nobody! Why would you poke your head into a door? That would hurt. But you'll never believe who poked his head into the door*way*.

It was Mr. Macky, our reading specialist! He had a scary-looking black strap in his hand.

"To what do we owe the pleasure of your company, Mr. Macky?" asked Mr. Granite.

That's grown-up talk for "What are *you* doing here?"

"The school reading scores are way down," Mr. Macky said. "So I'm forced to

take drastic action."

Mr. Macky and Mr. Granite told us they would be right back. Everybody had worried looks on their faces. We were all on pins and needles.

Well, not really. We were sitting on chairs. If we were on pins and needles, it would have hurt.

"Drastic action?" asked Emily, the big crybaby. "What do you think he's going to do?"

"He's probably going to whip us with that strap," said Michael, who never ties his shoes.

"Maybe he's going to strap us to our seats until our reading scores go up," said Ryan, who will eat anything, even stuff that isn't food.

"Whatever he does, it's Arlo's fault," said Andrea. She calls me by my real name because she knows I don't like it. "He probably flunked the reading test we took last week."

"Your *face* flunked the reading test," I said to Andrea.

I knew that didn't make any sense, but it was the first thing that came to my mind. It didn't matter, because Mr. Macky and Mr. Granite came back to the class. And this time they had company with them.

"EEEEEK!" Emily shrieked. "It's a *bear*!"

It sure looked like a bear, but it wasn't a bear. It was just the biggest dog in the history of the world. This dog was almost as big as Clifford the Big Red Dog. It was brown, and its tongue was hanging out. It was slobbering all over the place.

"Run for your lives!" shouted Neil, who we call the nude kid even though he wears clothes. "The bear is gonna eat us!"

Everybody freaked out and dived under their desks. I wasn't scared. I have a big dog named Buttons at home. But I dived under my desk anyway, just in case I was wrong and the dog *was* a bear.

"It's a *grizzly* bear!" shouted Alexia, this girl who rides a skateboard all the time.

"It's not a grizzly bear," Mr. Macky said as he attached the strap to the dog's collar. "It's a Labradoodle. That's a combination of a Labrador retriever and a poodle."

"It's a *grizzly* Labradoodle!" Alexia shouted.

"The grizzly Labradoodle is going to eat us!" Neil yelled. "Run for your lives!"

"Please calm down, everyone!" hollered Mr. Granite, who went over to pet the grizzly Labradoodle. "The dog is not going to hurt you. Look, it's friendly."

The Labradoodle sat on the floor while Mr. Granite petted it. It looked pretty tame to me. But once you start freaking out, it's hard to stop.

"I think grizzly Labradoodles have rabies!" shouted Alexia.

"It's a wild animal!" shouted Ryan.

"It's an attack Labradoodle!" hollered Michael.

"Help!" shouted Neil. "The giant, grizzly attack Labradoodle is going to bite my head off!"

"I'm afraid of dogs," whimpered Emily, who is afraid of everything. "I want my mommy!"

The rest of us started to come out from under our desks, but the dog barked and we all went back into hiding.

"I'll read better! I promise!" said Ryan. "Just take that man-eating Labradoodle away!"

"It's not a man-eating Labradoodle!" said Mr. Macky.

"Just take it away!" Michael shouted.

The giant, man-eating, grizzly attack Labradoodle barked again. It must have been a little freaked out by everybody freaking out. That made everybody freak out even *more*.

"EEEEEEEK!" Emily screamed.

"Help!" Alexia shouted. "I'm too young to die!"

It was hilarious. You should have been there.

The Amazing Miss Klute

We all made a run for the door to escape the giant, man-eating, grizzly attack Labradoodle before it could bite our heads off. But Mr. Macky wouldn't let us out of the room.

"Stop!" he shouted, holding up his hand like a traffic cop. "Everybody calm down.

The dog will not hurt you. She's here to help you with your reading."

WHAT?!

"How could a man-eating dog possibly help us with our reading?" asked Alexia.

"She's not a *man-eating* dog," Mr. Macky told us as he leaned over to scratch the dog's ears. "She's a *therapy* dog."

Therapy dog?

We all looked at each other. Not even Andrea knew what a "therapy dog" was, and Little Miss Know-It-All thinks she knows *everything*.

"What's a therapy dog?" asked Neil the nude kid.

"Therapy dogs are dogs that are trained

to help people," said Mr. Macky.

"So you want us to read . . . to a *dog*?" Ryan asked.

"Sure!" said Mr. Macky.

"And you think *that's* going to make us better readers?" asked Michael.

"Yes!"

Mr. Macky is wacky!*

Mr. Granite said that while we read to the dog, he would be in the teachers' lounge for a while. That's a secret room just for teachers where they can go to play video games, take a nap, or get a foot massage. My friend Billy, who lives around the corner, told me that the teachers' lounge

---

*Hey, that would make a good book title!

at his school has an all-you-can-eat buffet.

All-you-can-eat buffets are cool because you can eat as much as you want. That's why they're called all-you-can-eat buffets. They have the perfect name!

Hey, what if you went to one of those all-you-can-eat buffets and you just kept eating and eating and eating without stopping? I guess at some point they would tell you, "Okay, that's all you can eat. Now get out of here."

It would *still* have the perfect name!

I know that doesn't have anything to do with the story. The point is that Mr. Granite went to hang out in the teachers' lounge.

"It's against the rules to bring a dog to school," said Andrea, who probably has a poster in her room with all the rules on it so she can study them in her spare time.

"Therapy dogs *are* allowed in school," Mr. Macky told us. "Her name is Miss Klute. She's four years old, and she's really friendly, patient, calm, and gentle around people. Would you like to pet her?"

"I'm afraid," said Emily, of course.

"Miss Klute doesn't bite," said Mr. Macky. "She wouldn't hurt a fly."

"It's not flies I'm worried about," Emily said. "Does she bite girls? Girls named Emily?"

"Of course not!" Mr. Macky said. "She

loves people. And Miss Klute is even hypoallergenic. Does anybody know what hypoallergenic means?"

Andrea waved her hand in the air like she was stranded on a desert island and trying to signal a plane. But Mr. Macky called on me.

"That means Miss Klute is a kind of shampoo," I said, sticking my tongue out at Andrea. I knew that because my mom told me her shampoo is hypoallergenic.

"Not exactly, A.J.," said Mr. Macky. He called on Andrea.

"Hypoallergenic means Miss Klute won't bother people who are allergic to dogs," said Andrea.

"That's right, Andrea!"

Andrea smiled the smile that she smiles whenever she's the only one with the right answer. Why can't a truckload of hypo-allergenic shampoo fall on her head?

We all gathered around to pet Miss Klute. She seemed to like it. She didn't bite anybody's hand off, anyway.

"She's adorable!" announced Alexia.

"Miss Klute is cute!" said Emily.

18

"I love her!" Neil said, wrapping his arms around Miss Klute and hugging her.

Wow, a minute ago Neil thought Miss Klute was going to bite his head off, and now he was saying he loved her. Neil is weird.

"Would you like me to read a story to Miss Klute?" asked Mr. Macky.

"Yes!" said all the girls.

"No!" said all the boys.

I still didn't get it. Dogs don't understand English. Why would anybody want to read to them? Boy, for a reading specialist, Mr. Macky didn't know a whole lot about reading.

He pulled a book off the shelf. It was

called *Doug Unplugged*. Mr. Macky sat on the floor next to Miss Klute, and we all gathered around him.

"This is Doug. He's a robot," read Mr. Macky. *"Each morning his parents plug him in to fill him up with lots and lots of facts."*

I looked at Miss Klute. She was looking at Mr. Macky as he read.

"They love their little robot and want him to be the smartest robot ever," Mr. Macky read from the book.

Miss Klute cuddled herself up into a giant ball and put her head on Mr. Macky's lap as he read about Doug the robot. I had to admit, it *was* adorable.

Doug Unplugged was a cool story. It had us all glued to our seats.

Well, not really. We were sitting on the floor. Why would anybody glue themselves to a seat? How would you get the glue off?

When he got to the middle of the story, Mr. Macky reached into his pocket and pulled out a Cheerio. He gave it to Miss Klute to eat.

"You keep Cheerios in your *pocket*?" I asked. "That's weird."

"Did you run out of bowls?" asked Ryan.

"No, we had to put Miss Klute on a special diet," Mr. Macky said, "because sometimes she eats too much."

"My mom is on a special diet," I said. "If she loses ten pounds, she's going to buy a bikini."

"Your mom is weird," said Michael.

"If Miss Klute loses ten pounds, we should get *her* a bikini," suggested Ryan.

"Yeah, Miss Klute would look good in a bikini," said Neil.

"Dogs don't wear bikinis!" said Alexia.

"That's right," Emily said. "They go swimming naked."

"Ewww, disgusting!" we all shouted.

"Let's stay on task, shall we?" said Mr. Macky.

He finished reading *Doug Unplugged*. Then he gave Miss Klute another Cheerio.

"It looked like she was really paying attention to the story," Andrea said. "Miss Klute is amazing!"

No, she's not. She just sat there and did nothing the whole time. Do you know what would *really* be amazing? If Miss Klute read a story to *us*.

Now *that* would be amazing.

The Magical Teachers' Lounge

Mr. Macky said he had to leave because he needed to bring Miss Klute to the other classes. But the next day, after we finished math, he poked his head into our doorway again.

"Miss Klute is here!" everybody yelled when we saw her. "Hooray!"

"Would you like to read her a story?" Mr. Macky asked.

"Yeah!" said all the girls.

"Yeah!" said all the boys.

Mr. Granite told us he would be in the teachers' lounge for a while. I think I want to be a teacher when I grow up. That way I can go hang out in the teachers' lounge all day and get foot massages.

"Is it true that the teachers' lounge has a minibar filled with candy?" Michael asked Mr. Granite before he left.

"I heard that in the teachers' lounge they have servants on roller skates who feed you grapes and give you back rubs," said Ryan.

"That's true," Mr. Granite told us. "And there are hundred-dollar bills scattered all over the floor, too. You can just scoop them up and keep them."

"WOW," we all said, which is "MOM" upside down.

"What do you do with the hundred-dollar bills?" I asked Mr. Granite.

"We use them for toilet paper," he told us.

Ewww, disgusting!

I think Mr. Granite was yanking our chain. Nobody would *ever* use hundred-dollar bills for toilet paper. You would use *one*-dollar bills.

Mr. Macky sat on the rug in the corner

with Miss Klute, and we all gathered around them. Mr. Macky had a book called *Uncle Willie and the Soup Kitchen*. It was about a guy named Uncle Willie who works in a soup kitchen. So it has the perfect name!

Mr. Macky read the first sentence in the book, and then he passed the book over to Andrea. She read a sentence and then she passed the book over to Ryan. He read a sentence and passed the book over to Michael. Each of us got the chance to read part of the story. It was cool.

No matter who was reading, Miss Klute sat and listened. Sometimes she would stare at the kid who was reading. It looked like she was really following the story. Other times she curled up in a big ball and rested her giant head on somebody's leg.

While one of us was reading, the rest of us would pet Miss Klute's ears, hold her paws, and feed her Cheerios. Sometimes kids grabbed her too hard or even pinched her. But Miss Klute never barked or snapped or growled. She didn't care what we did to her.

Mr. Macky was right about one thing. It's more fun to read when you're reading to a dog. Some of us made mistakes, but nobody laughed. Certainly not Miss Klute. Dogs never make fun of you when you make mistakes.

After we finished the story, Mr. Macky said he and Miss Klute had to go read with another class.

"No! Don't go!" everybody started yelling. "We want to read another story to Miss Klute!"

"Boo!"

"Please please please *please* don't go," I begged.

If you ever want something really badly, just say "please" over and over again to a grown-up. That's the first rule of being a kid.

"I thought you *hated* reading out loud, A.J.," said Mr. Macky.

"I do," I told him. "But reading is more fun when we read to Miss Klute. Please please please . . ."

"Well, as a reading specialist, I can't resist *that*," he said. "Okay, we can read *one* more story to Miss Klute."

"Yay!" everybody yelled.

I tell you, it works every time.

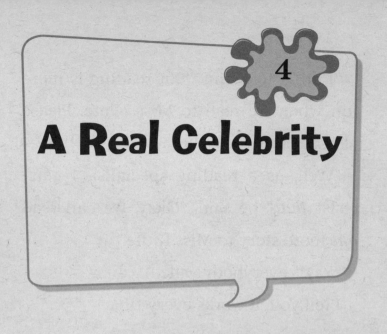

A Real Celebrity

After a few days nobody was afraid of Miss Klute anymore. Not even Emily, and she's afraid of *everything*. Our principal, Mr. Klutz, said Miss Klute had become part of the Ella Mentry School family. She came to school every day. When she wasn't having kids read to her, her job was "hall patrol." That meant she would walk up and down the hallway. Sometimes she would pop into our class.

Miss Klute was like a real celebrity at school. We asked Mr. Macky if we could have her autograph, so he copied a bunch of paw prints and passed them out to everyone. He also trained Miss Klute to do a cool trick. When we came into the front door in the morning, she was waiting for us. If you waved to her, she would put one paw in the air and move it back and forth. It looked just like she was waving back at you!

Wednesday was Funny Hat Day, and somebody gave Miss Klute a pair of antlers to wear. It was hilarious. You could do just about *anything* to her. She didn't mind.

Miss Klute is a hoot!

The day after Funny Hat Day was Emily's birthday. We all had to be nice to her, which was gross. But the best part was that Emily's mom brought in chocolate cupcakes for the whole class.* I *love* cupcakes, and my favorite flavor is chocolate. So it's a win-win! I would eat chocolate cupcakes

---

*Cupcakes have the perfect name because they're cakes in cups. If you ask me, doughnuts should be nuts in dough.

for breakfast, lunch, and dinner if my mom would let me. There were plenty of extra cupcakes, but Mr. Granite said we could only have one each. Bummer in the summer!

Right after we sang "Happy Birthday" to Emily, you'll never believe who walked into the door.

Nobody! It would hurt if you walked into a door. I thought we went over that

already. But you'll never believe who walked into the door*way*.

It was Mr. Macky and Miss Klute!

"Hooray! Miss Klute is here!" we all shouted.

Mr. Macky was carrying a book called *The Fuzzy Little Bunny*. We cleared off our desks and went to sit on the rug in the corner of the class with Miss Klute.

"I'll be in the teachers' lounge," said Mr. Granite, taking the extra cupcakes with him.

Lucky stiff! What could be better than sitting in the greatest place in the world and eating chocolate cupcakes?

We were all petting Miss Klute and

rubbing her ears.

"Okay, whose turn is it to start reading today?" asked Mr. Macky.

"Mine!" everybody shouted.

We all wanted to be the first to read, because Miss Klute usually cuddles up to the first reader and stays there.

"I want to read to Miss Klute first!" shouted Andrea.

"You started last time!" Neil said. "It's my turn!"

"I was absent last time," said Michael. "I didn't get to read to Miss Klute at all."

"That's not our problem," said Ryan.

"Miss Klute told me she wants *me* to read to her first," I said, even though that totally wasn't true.

"She did not!" said Alexia. "She can't even talk."

"Well, she was *thinking* it."

Everybody was yelling, shouting, and arguing. I thought there was going to be a riot in there!

"It's Emily's birthday," Andrea finally said. "*She* should get to read to Miss Klute first."

"That's a good point, Andrea," Mr. Macky said. "I would like Emily to start our reading."

Mr. Macky gave Emily *The Fuzzy Little Bunny.* She looked at the book for a few seconds, and then she closed it. There

were tears in her eyes.

"What's wrong, Emily?" asked Mr. Macky.

"I don't want to read."

"Why not?"

"Because."

"Because why?"

Mr. Macky finally got Emily to tell him why she didn't want to read. She said it really softly. . . .

"Because *you're* here," she whispered.

"Ohhhhhh!" said Mr. Macky. "Okay, it's Emily's birthday, so I'll leave you kids alone and come back in fifteen minutes to see how you're making out."

"Ewww! Gross!" we all yelled, because

Mr. Macky said "making out."

"I'll be in the teachers' lounge," he said.

"Can I come, too?" I asked. "I want another cupcake."

"No!"

The Fuzzy Little Bunny

Mr. Macky told us to be on our best behavior while he was in the teachers' lounge. So as soon as he left the room, Alexia, Ryan, and I got up and shook our butts at the class.

"Woo-hoo," shouted Ryan. "The grown-ups are gone!"

"We can do anything we want!" hollered Alexia.

"This is the greatest day of my life," I yelled.

Andrea and Emily were rolling their eyes and making mean faces at us.

"Miss Klute is a grown-up, you know," Andrea said. "She's four years old. That's thirty-two in dog years."

"Yes," said Emily. "Miss Klute hears every word you're saying. Maybe she'll report back to Mr. Macky, and you'll get in trouble."

"What's she gonna tell him?" I asked. "*Bow-wow*? *Arf, arf*? *Woof*?"

Miss Klute was staring at us the whole

time. It looked like she was really listening to our conversation.

"I guess we'd better start reading," Ryan said. "Just in case."

Alexia, Ryan, and I went back to the corner and sat on the rug. Emily started to read from *The Fuzzy Little Bunny*.

"It was a lovely summer day," she read, *"and the fuzzy little bunny went hip hop hopping down the road. It was Monday, and that meant her mommy was going to cook up a big pot of blah blah blah blah blah blah blah blah blah blah blah blah blah blah blah blah blah blah blah blah . . ."*

The Fuzzy Little Bunny was the most boring book in the history of the world!

I thought I might die from old age before the story was done. Miss Klute rested her head on Emily's lap and closed her eyes.

"She looks bored out of her mind," said Neil the nude kid.

"Maybe Miss Klute doesn't like *The Fuzzy Little Bunny*," said Alexia.

"I can't blame her," Ryan said. "That story is lame."

"I might fall asleep myself," said Michael. "I've heard this story before. The only thing that happens is that the fuzzy little bunny gets to eat a carrot at the end. Big deal."

"What a snoozefest," I said.

"I *like* the story of *The Fuzzy Little*

Bunny," said Andrea.

"Me too," said Emily, who agrees with everything Andrea says.

That's when I came up with the greatest idea in the history of the world.

"It's my turn to read," I said, taking the book from Emily.

I flipped to the next page and started to read. Well, I *pretended* to read anyway. . . .

"After that," I said, "the fuzzy little bunny went to the skate shop and bought a rocket-powered antigravity skateboard, with dual torpedoes on each side. It was *awesome*. The fuzzy little bunny had always dreamed about jumping a skateboard over the Grand Canyon."

"That's not what it says, Arlo!" said Andrea. "You made all that up."

"So what?" I said. "Miss Klute won't know the difference. She's a dog. Maybe she'll like the story better this way."

I passed the book over to Ryan, and he began to "read."

"So the fuzzy little bunny got on her rocket skateboard and started to jump over the Grand Canyon," Ryan read. "But little did she know that on the other side of the Grand Canyon a fuzzy little *kitten* was taking off on a rocket skateboard at the very same time!"

Hey, this story was getting cool! I looked over at Miss Klute. She was just sitting there listening, like always.

Ryan passed the book over to Michael, and he began to "read."

"So the fuzzy little bunny and the fuzzy little kitten realized they were going to crash into each other over the Grand Canyon!" Michael read. "So they both turned on their laser beams and started shooting at each other! *Bam bam bam bam!*"

Wow! I couldn't wait to find out what happened next! This was the most exciting story in the history of the world!

Andrea rolled her eyes. Miss Klute just sat there, listening.

Michael passed the book over to Alexia, and she began to "read."

"And then the fuzzy little bunny caught on fire! She was falling into the Grand Canyon! It looked like it was all over for her. Unless . . ."

"Unless *what*?" I asked Alexia. "Did the fuzzy little kitten rescue the fuzzy little bunny?"

Miss Klute just sat there. She didn't seem to care a bit what happened to the fuzzy little bunny.

Alexia passed the book over to Neil the nude kid, and he began to "read."

"And then aliens came from outer space!" read Neil. "They had four eyeballs, six noses, and laser cannons instead of arms."

"Laser cannons are *cool*!" I shouted.

Miss Klute just sat there. If aliens shooting laser cannons doesn't get you excited, I guess *nothing* gets you excited.

"What happened next?" we all begged Neil.

"Yeah, what happened next?" asked Alexia.

Neil didn't seem to know what happened next. He thought about it for a minute.

"And then the earth exploded and everybody died," he finally said. "The end."

Neil closed *The Fuzzy Little Bunny*. Miss Klute just sat there.

"You can't say the earth exploded and everybody died," Andrea shouted. "It's a book for *children*!"*

"So what?" I shouted back at Andrea. "You can say whatever you want!"

"Can not!" she shouted back.

We could have gone on like that for a while, but Mr. Granite and Mr. Macky came back to class.

"So how are you kids making out with *The Fuzzy Little Bunny*?" Mr. Granite asked us.

"Ewwww! Gross!" everybody shouted. "We're not making out with the fuzzy little bunny!"

"Did you like the story?" asked Mr. Macky.

---

*Send your angry emails to: lightenup@getasenseof-humortransplant.com.

"Oh, yeah!" we all shouted.

"*The Fuzzy Little Bunny* is *awesome*!" said Alexia.

"What was your favorite part?" asked Mr. Macky.

Everybody raised their hands except for me, of course. So naturally, Mr. Macky called on me.

"I liked the part where they turned on their laser beams and started shooting at each other," I said.

"Yeah, that was cool," agreed Ryan.

"Hmm," said Mr. Macky, opening *The Fuzzy Little Bunny* and leafing through the pages. "I don't seem to remember *that* part."

My Brilliant Idea

Every day, Miss Klute has to do "lunch duty." That means she walks around the vomitorium looking for scraps that fell on the floor so she can eat them. Miss Klute is like a vacuum cleaner for food! She'll even eat stuff that Ryan won't eat. Sometimes kids drop their lunch on purpose just to watch Miss Klute run over and scoop it up.

"Where do you think Mr. Macky got a therapy dog?" asked Michael.

"From Rent-A-Therapy Dog," I told him. "You can rent anything."

On Emily's birthday it was Hot Dog Day in the vomitorium. Me and the gang were eating lunch and minding our own business when Little Miss Perfect and the crybaby birthday girl sat down at our table with their trays. Emily went to get a mustard packet, and in that second or two the most amazing thing in the history of the world happened.

Miss Klute grabbed the hot dog right off her plate!

"Hey, where did my hot dog go?" Emily said when she got back to the table.

Then we saw Miss Klute walking in the other direction with a hot dog sticking out of her mouth. It was hilarious.

"Miss Klute stole my hot dog!" Emily shouted. "And it's my birthday! We've got to *do* something!"

Then she started crying and ran out of the vomitorium.

Sheesh, get a grip! What a crybaby.

After we all stopped laughing, I noticed that Andrea had on her worried face.

"Don't worry," I told her. "Emily will get another hot dog."

"That's not what I'm worried about,"

Andrea said. "I'm concerned about Miss Klute."

"What about her?" asked Michael.

"Whenever we have reading time, she just lies there."

"So what?" said Alexia. "Maybe she's tired."

"Why should she be tired?" asked Ryan. "All she does is eat and listen to kids read all day."

"She seems so sad," said Andrea. "She's got such a hangdog look on her face."

"She's a *dog*," I said. "She's *supposed* to have a hangdog look on her face."

"My mother is a psychologist," Andrea said. "She told me that Miss Klute has all the classic signs of depression."

"What?!" Neil said. "Dogs don't get depressed."

"How do *you* know?" Andrea replied. "Maybe dogs are just like people, but with paws and fur."

"Are you saying that our therapy dog needs therapy?" asked Alexia.

"She might," Andrea replied. "I think we should try to cheer her up."

Maybe Andrea was right. Miss Klute did look kind of sad most of the time.

After lunch we decided to skip recess and go to Mr. Macky's office instead. Miss Klute was sitting on the floor in there, looking sad as usual.

"What can I do for you kids?" Mr. Macky asked us.

"Can we be alone with Miss Klute for a few minutes?" asked Andrea.

"How come?" asked Mr. Macky.

"We have to tell her something," I explained. "It's personal. Please? Please? Please?"

"Uh, okay, I guess," Mr. Macky said. "I'll be in the teachers' lounge."

"Okay, what are we gonna do to cheer Miss Klute up?" Ryan asked after Mr. Macky left.

"We could tell her jokes," suggested Alexia. "You know lots of them, A.J. Go ahead, tell her one."

"Okay," I said, getting down on the floor next to Miss Klute's ear. "Do you know why the skeleton didn't go to the school dance?"

"Why?" everybody asked.

"He had no body to go with," I said.

We all looked at Miss Klute. She just sat there, looking sad.

"Try another joke, A.J.," said Neil.

"Okay," I said. "Do you know which football team travels with the most luggage? The Green Bay Packers! Get it? Luggage? Packers?"

Miss Klute just sat there, looking sad.

"She really *is* depressed," I said. "Those are my best jokes."

"Do you know any *dog* jokes?" Andrea asked. "Maybe she needs jokes she can relate to."

"Okay," I said. "How are dogs and marine biologists alike?"

"How?" everybody asked.

"One wags her tail, and the other tags her whale."

Miss Klute just sat there, looking sad.

"What kind of dog does Dracula have?" I said.

"What kind?" everybody asked.

"A bloodhound."

Miss Klute just sat there, looking sad.

"What do you get if you cross a cocker spaniel, a poodle, and a rooster?" I said.

"What?" everybody asked.

"A cockerpoodledoo!"

Miss Klute just sat there, looking sad.

"Those jokes are *horrible*, Arlo," Andrea said. "I think you made her even more depressed than she was before."

"Well, if you're so smart, let's see *you* try to cheer her up," I told Andrea.

"Maybe she would like it if I danced for her," suggested Andrea. "I just started taking Irish step-dancing classes after school."

Andrea takes classes in *everything* after

school. If they gave a class in nose pick-
ing, she would probably take that class so
she would get better at it.

We all rolled our eyes as Andrea danced
around Mr. Macky's office. It was weird.
And it didn't seem to have any effect on
Miss Klute. She just sat there staring at
Andrea.

"See? You can't cheer her up either," I
said.

"Maybe she doesn't *want* to be a therapy dog," said Alexia. "Did you ever think
of that? Maybe she wants to be a Seeing
Eye dog."

"Or a firehouse dog," said Neil. "That
would be cool."

"Maybe she wishes she was a cat," I said.

"Poor Miss Klute," Ryan said, wrapping his arms around her. "She's cooped up in here all day long. Dogs don't need to know how to read, write, or do math. They don't want to go to school."

"Maybe she just wants to go outside," I suggested.

"That's it!" said Andrea, snapping her fingers. "You're a genius!"

"Ooooo!" Ryan said. "Andrea called A.J. a genius. They must be in *love*!"

"When are you gonna get married?" asked Michael.

If those guys weren't my best friends, I would hate them.

Chess for Dogs

A few minutes later, Mr. Macky came back from the teachers' lounge. Emily was with him, eating a hot dog.

"So how are you making out with Miss Klute?" Mr. Macky asked.

"Ewwww! Gross!" we all shouted. "We're not making out with Miss Klute!"

"Arlo had a great idea," Andrea said. "Go ahead; ask him, Arlo."

"Mr. Macky, can we take Miss Klute outside for recess?" I asked.

"Gee, I don't know," Mr. Macky replied. "Miss Klute is trained to be an *indoor* therapy dog."

"Please please please please please please please please please!" we all begged.

"I suppose Miss Klute *could* use a little fresh air," said Mr. Macky. "Well, okay."

"Yay!"

Like I said, that *please please please* thing works every time. It really *is* a magic word.

Mr. Macky hooked Miss Klute's leash to

her collar and said we could take her outside until recess was over.

"Which one of you is the most responsible?" he asked.

"I am!" we all shouted.*

"It was A.J.'s idea to take Miss Klute outside," said Michael.

"Okay," Mr. Macky said, handing me the leash. "Be careful with her."

"I will," I promised.

When we got out to the playground, all the other kids came running over.

"Miss Klute is here!" everybody shouted. "Hi Miss Klute!"

---

*I knew that I was responsible, because when I'm home and something goes wrong, my mom always says, "A.J., you're responsible!"

It was like she was the queen of the playground. Everybody wanted to pet her and hug her. We walked Miss Klute around and showed her the monkey bars, the swings, and the slide. She looked pretty happy.

"See?" I said. "She *likes* being outside!"

I should get the No Bell Prize for that idea. That's a prize they give out to people who don't have bells.

Miss Klute was pulling at the leash, and I had to run to keep up with her. She was pretty fast for a big dog.

"Hey, maybe we should play fetch," I said, stopping to catch my breath.

"I don't know if that's a good idea, Arlo,"

Andrea said. "Mr. Macky didn't say it was okay to let Miss Klute run around without holding her leash."

"He didn't say it *wasn't* okay either," I told Andrea. "He just said to be careful with her."

Fetch is a simple game. You throw something, and the dog runs to get it. Then she brings it back and you throw it again. It seems like a pretty dumb game, if you ask me. But I guess playing fetch is like chess for dogs.

There was a tennis ball in the grass. I let go of Miss Klute's leash and threw the ball toward the soccer field.

"Go get it, girl!" I shouted.

Miss Klute took off, running like the wind.

"Look at her go!" Ryan yelled.

It was amazing! Miss Klute chased down the ball and caught it in her mouth even before it stopped bouncing. Then she ran back and dropped the ball at my feet.

"Good girl!" we all said, petting Miss Klute.

She was panting, and her tongue was hanging out.

"Do it again, A.J.!" Neil said.

I threw the ball a little farther this time, and Miss Klute took off after it. Again, she grabbed it in her mouth and brought it back to me. She looked like she wanted me to throw it again, so I did. She dashed off to get it.

"Miss Klute sure likes to run!" shouted Ryan.

"She's having so much fun!" yelled Alexia.

"I think she just wanted to play," said Michael.

"I've never seen her so happy!" shouted Andrea.

That's when the weirdest thing in the history of the world happened. A squirrel ran out onto the soccer field.

Well, that's not the weird part, because squirrels run out onto soccer fields all the time. The weird part was what

happened *next*.

Miss Klute saw the squirrel run in front of her. I guess that squirrel was a lot more interesting than the tennis ball. So Miss Klute changed direction and ran after the squirrel instead of the ball!

The squirrel must have freaked out when it saw that giant, bear-sized dog chasing it. It changed direction and headed for the woods next to the playground!

Miss Klute followed the squirrel!

The two of them disappeared into the woods!

"Where did she go?" asked Ryan.

I looked at Ryan. Ryan looked at Michael. Michael looked at Alexia. Alexia

looked at Neil. Neil looked at Andrea.
Andrea looked at me. Then we all looked
at the woods.

Miss Klute was *gone*!

The Worst Day of My Life

"What are we gonna do?" I shouted. "We have to find Miss Klute!"

"*You* have to find Miss Klute, Arlo," Andrea said. "You're the one who lost her."

"Oh, man, you're in trouble, A.J.," said Ryan. "If Miss Klute doesn't come back, you'll probably be suspended for the rest of your life."

Hmmm, I thought, trying to figure out if that was a good thing or a bad thing.

"No, they'll probably just lock A.J. up in the dungeon on the third floor," said Michael.

"I *told* you not to let Miss Klute run around without a leash, Arlo," Andrea said. "Now she's gone, and it's all *your* fault."

Every time I do something wrong, Andrea has a little smile on her face. What is her problem?

Riiiiinnnnnggggg!

Oh no! It was the bell. Recess was over.

I looked toward the woods one more time, hoping to see Miss Klute come running out. But she didn't. Everybody went inside the school. I was the last one to come in. Mr. Macky was waiting for me in the hallway.

"Who is holding Miss Klute?" he asked. "Did she like being outside?"

"I guess so," I told him. "She's still out there, somewhere."

"What!?"

Mr. Macky's eyes were bugging out of his head like golf balls.

"We were playing fetch," I explained, "and a squirrel ran by. Miss Klute took off after the squirrel. They both went running into the woods. And that was the last we saw her."

Mr. Macky looked like one of those cartoon characters who gets really mad and smoke pours out of their ears.

"I told you to take good care of her!" he yelled.

"I did!" I said. "She was having a great time, right up until the moment she ran away."

"We have to find her!" Mr. Macky said. Then he went running down the hall toward the front office.

A few seconds later, an announcement came over the loudspeaker.

"All students and teachers! Report to the playground immediately! Miss Klute is missing!"

A second after that, everybody poured out of their classrooms yelling and screaming and freaking out.

"Miss Klute is missing!"

"Where is she?"

"We have to find her!"

What happened next was the biggest manhunt in the history of the world. Or doghunt anyway. The whole school—kids and grown-ups—ran out into the woods by the playground. We were all searching for Miss Klute.

"Yoo-hoo! Miss Klute, where are you?" everybody was shouting.

Mr. Macky was walking around the woods with binoculars. Our security guard, Officer Spence, was searching for clues with a magnifying glass. Our science teacher, Mr. Docker, was wearing night vision goggles. Our art teacher, Ms. Hannah, was putting up MISSING posters with Miss Klute's picture on them. Our computer teacher, Mrs. Yonkers, was holding up some weird machine that said DOG DETECTOR on it.

Our librarian, Mrs. Roopy, passed out books to all the kids. She told us that if we were reading, Miss Klute might come out of her hiding place.

A few minutes later, a helicopter was hovering overhead. Mrs. Lilly, a reporter from the local newspaper, showed up in a

van with a camera crew. She ran over to interview Mr. Macky.

"Why did your therapy dog run away?" asked Mrs. Lilly. "Did you beat her? Did you starve her? Does she have rabies? Did she bite somebody? Are you part of a dogfighting ring? What do you know, and when did you know it? My readers want to know the truth."

"We'll find Miss Klute," Mr. Macky told her, "if it's the *last* thing we do."

But after an hour or so of searching all over the woods, we still hadn't found Miss Klute. It was hopeless.

"Well, I guess Miss Klute isn't coming back," said Principal Klutz. "Let's go

inside, everyone."

Some of the kids were crying. I saw some other kids whispering and pointing at me. They knew it was my fault.

This was the worst thing to happen to me since TV Turnoff Week. Miss Klute had run away. And now I wanted to run away to Antarctica and go live with the penguins. Bummer in the summer!

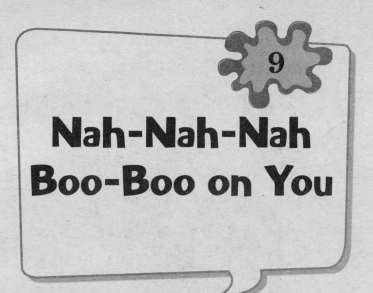

Nah-Nah-Nah
Boo-Boo on You

As we filed back inside the school, every-one looked depressed.

"I can't believe this happened on my birthday," said Emily. "Why do bad things always happen to *me*?"

Soon it would be three o'clock, when we go home for the day. Mr. Klutz

announced that classes were canceled for the rest of the afternoon. He told us to go to the all-purpose room so we could talk about our feelings and stuff.

At first nobody said anything. But then

kids started to say what was on their mind.

"Before Miss Klute came to our school, I didn't like to read," said Neil the nude kid. "Now reading is my favorite thing to do in the world."

"Me too," said a bunch of kids.

"She was so nice," said Alexia. "She never snarled or bit or hurt anybody."

"She was my best friend," said Ryan.

Everybody was sobbing. Even some of the teachers were pulling out handkerchiefs and wiping their eyes with them.

"Miss Klute was the best therapy dog I ever met," said Mr. Macky.

"I'm sorry," I told everybody. "This was all my fault."

"Don't be so hard on yourself, A.J.," said Mr. Macky. "It could have happened to anybody."

After that nobody said anything for a million hundred seconds. There was just the sound of sobbing and sniffling.

"I miss Miss Klute," Andrea finally said.

"I miss miss Miss Klute," said Alexia.

"I miss miss miss Miss Klute," said Michael.

It went on like that for a while. That's when the most amazing thing in the history of the world happened.

Oh, yeah, I know what you're thinking. You're thinking that Miss Klute came running into the all-purpose room, all

happy and everything. You're thinking
that we all started cheering and hugging
her. You're thinking that everybody lived
happily ever after.

Well, that's not what happened. So nah-nah-nah boo-boo on you!

This is what *really* happened. . . .

Somebody down the hallway let out a scream!

EEEEEEEEEEEEKKKKKK!

It was a lady's scream.

"That came from the teachers' lounge!" Ryan yelled.

We all ran out of the all-purpose room and down the hall to the teachers' lounge.

The school secretary, Miss Patty, was standing in front of the door.

"Miss Klute is DEAD!" she shouted.

The Truth about the Teachers' Lounge

Okay, Miss Klute wasn't *really* dead. So stop freaking out. And don't bother writing angry letters and emails to the publisher of this book.

She wasn't dead, but she *was* pretty sick. Miss Klute was lying in the middle of the teachers' lounge, hardly moving. Worse than that, she had thrown up all over the floor. Ugh, gross! And we saw it live and in person. I thought I was gonna die.

Our school nurse, Mrs. Cooney, came running in.

"What happened?" she asked.

"Miss Klute must have come back to school while we were out looking for her in the woods," Andrea told her.

Mrs. Cooney got down on her knees and listened to Miss Klute's heartbeat. Then she picked a little piece of paper off the floor.

"Aha! Here's the problem!" she said. "It's a cupcake wrapper. Where did Miss Klute get chocolate cupcakes?"

We all looked at Emily.

"I killed Miss Klute!" Emily shouted. And then she started crying and went running out of the room. "This is the worst birthday I ever had!"

What a crybaby.

"Is Miss Klute going to be okay?" Andrea asked Mrs. Cooney.

"I think so," she replied. "But she might have to go to the animal hospital for a few days to recover. They'll make sure she doesn't eat any more chocolate."

I thought *everybody* knew dogs can't eat chocolate. That's the first rule of being a dog.

Our school custodian, Miss Lazar, came into the teachers' lounge. She looked at the floor.

"Have no fear!" said Miss Lazar. "This looks like a job for Super Custodian!"

"Miss Klute got sick," said Mrs. Cooney. "It's quite a mess, I'm afraid."

"The messier the better," said Miss Lazar. "I love messes! If there weren't any messes, I wouldn't have a job."

Miss Lazar is bizarre.*

"Stand aside," said Miss Lazar. "Super Custodian is here to save the day! Any time finger paint is spilled, or the toilets become clogged, or somebody throws up, I am at your service to—"

"Can you just clean up the mess, please?" asked Mrs. Cooney.

"You can count on me!" Miss Lazar replied.

She put on these big, yellow plastic gloves and started cleaning up the mess.

---

*Hey, that would make a good book title, too!

It was gross. Mrs. Cooney told us to go back to our classroom.

That's when I realized something. I looked around the teachers' lounge. Where was the hot tub? Where were the video games? There was no minibar filled with candy or an all-you-can-eat buffet. There were no servants on roller skates giving out foot massages and back rubs. And there wasn't a single hundred-dollar bill on the floor!

That's when I decided that I didn't want to be a teacher after all. I had thought the teachers' lounge was this really cool place where the teachers can hang out all day and do cool stuff. But it's just a boring

old room with tables, chairs, and a cof-
fee machine. It's no fun at all. Plus, you
never know when a dog might come in
and throw up all over the place.

A week later we came into our classroom,
and you'll never believe in a million hundred years who was sitting on the floor
chewing on a chew toy.

It was Miss Klute!

Well, it would have been pretty weird
if anybody *else* was sitting on the floor
chewing on a chew toy.

Mr. Macky told us that Miss Klute was
all better. The whole class ran over to hug
and pet her.

"We missed you!" said Andrea.

"Why did you run away?" Ryan asked.

"Did you have fun chasing that squirrel in the woods?" asked Alexia.

"Did you have fun eating Emily's cupcakes and throwing up all over the teachers' lounge?" I asked.

Miss Klute didn't answer any of our questions, because she's a DOG. Duh! But she did let us hug her and pet her for a long time. And then Mr. Macky let us read her a story about a dog that ran away.

Maybe after this they'll get a hot tub and some other cool stuff for the teachers' lounge. Maybe I'll go to an all-you-can-eat

buffet for dinner tonight. Maybe my mom will stop using hypoallergenic shampoo. Maybe Miss Klute will lose ten pounds and get a bikini. Maybe Mr. Macky will put his cereal in a bowl instead of carrying it around in his pockets. Maybe the teachers will stop using money for toilet paper. Maybe aliens will use their laser cannons to save the fuzzy little bunny from falling into the Grand Canyon. Maybe Miss Klute will stop stealing hot dogs from kids' lunch trays. Maybe somebody will cross a cocker spaniel, a poodle, and a rooster to make a cockerpoodledoo. Maybe we can talk Mr. Macky into letting us take Miss Klute outside for recess again.

But it won't be easy!